W9-ATK-072

# Katharine the Almost Great

# Uses Her Common Cents

by Lisa Mullarkey

illustrated by Phyllis Harris

magic
wagon

**visit us at www.abdopublishing.com**

*To Jan, Stephanie, and Phyllis*
*for their help in bringing Katharine to life —LM*

*To Lily, Mia, and Drew, my wonderful nieces—PH*

Published by Magic Wagon, a division of the ABDO Group, 8000 West
78th Street, Edina, Minnesota, 55439. Copyright © 2009 by Abdo
Consulting Group, Inc. International copyrights reserved in all countries.
All rights reserved. No part of this book may be reproduced in any form
without written permission from the publisher.

Calico Chapter Books™ is a trademark and logo of Magic Wagon.

Printed in the United States.

Text by Lisa Mullarkey
Illustrations by Phyllis Harris
Edited by Stephanie Hedlund and Rochelle Baltzer
Interior layout and design by Jaime Martens
Cover design by Jaime Martens

**Library of Congress Cataloging-in-Publication Data**

Mullarkey, Lisa.
  Uses her common cents / by Lisa Mullarkey ; illustrated by Phyllis Harris.
     p. cm. -- (Katharine the almost great ; bk. 1)
  ISBN 978-1-60270-579-1
  [1. Moneymaking projects--Fiction. 2. Schools--Fiction.] I. Harris,
Phyllis, 1962- ill. II. Title.
  PZ7.M91148Use 2009
  [E]--dc22
                                    2008036101

# ❋ CONTENTS ❋

# ❁ CHAPTER 1 ❁

## *The Tattoo Queen*

I had a total ick day. A make-me-feel-sick day. A crumple-it-up-and-give-it-a-kick day.

My cousin Crockett has a calendar that lists special holidays around the world. Not just mega holidays like Christmas but super secret holidays like Take Your Houseplant for a Walk Day, Give an Apple to Your Teacher Day, and Talk Like a Pirate Day. On Fridays, Crockett brings the calendar to recess and lets our whole third grade class take a sneaky peek. Crockett said today was Dare to Be Different Day.

So at breakfast, instead of eating my usual bowl of cereal, I dared to be different. I spied a can of cream soda in the fridge. Cream soda's practically milk, isn't it? I drizzled it over my Crispies and watched them swirl before sinking.

After the first spoonful, my taste buds freaked out. Maybe I'm not a dare-to-be-different girl after all.

Before my mom woke up, I dumped the bowl into the trash. If she knew cereal à la soda was on my menu, there'd be major mama drama.

I bolted upstairs to brush the grungy taste out of my mouth. After two seconds, I knew something was wrong.

*Diaper rash ointment!* Yuck! I spit into the sink and grabbed the minty-fresh mouthwash to get rid of the disgust-o taste.

Things were looking up at school when my teacher, Mrs. Bingsley, made an announcement.

"Our class is responsible for the school-wide service project next month," she said. She tapped the character education poster on the board and turned to Vanessa Garfinkle, aka Miss Priss-A-Poo. "Wasn't your family in charge of the car wash last year, Vanessa?"

Vanessa stood and bowed. "We raised the most money EV-er." Her nose shot into the air on *EV-er*.

"Let's try to raise just as much this year," said Mrs. Bingsley. "Let's work together and brainstorm ideas. On Monday, we'll vote for our favorite."

I raced over to the best thinking spot in the class: the purplicious beanbag chair in the art center. But Miss Priss-A-Poo the Car Wash Queen beat me to it.

"Well, got any ideas?" asked Miss Priss-A-Poo as she scribbled *Vanessa's Brilliant Ideas* on her paper.

I had to think fast. A marker caught my eye. "I'm going to draw tattoos and charge a buck each. I'm a fab-u-lo-so artist, you know."

Miss Priss-A-Poo smirked. "Oh, does your mom put all your pictures in gold frames and hang them in your house, too?"

I ignored her. "My super-duper tattoos will raise way more money than your car wash."

Crockett squeezed in next to me and rolled up his sleeve.

"Arrr," he said. "I'll take a tattoo, matey." He must think today is Talk Like a Pirate Day.

I grabbed a marker and sketched a pirate on his arm. He gave it two thumbs-up.

But I didn't stop there. I added an earring, stubble on his chin, and a pirate patch.

Johnny Mazzaratti crawled over to have a peek-a-roo. Johnny, Crockett, and I have been friends since first grade. That's when Crockett and I volunteered to sit with Johnny at the peanut-free snack table.

"Can I have one?" Johnny asked. Two minutes later, he was the spittin' image of a pirate from the Caribbean.

Miss Priss-A-Poo studied the tattoos. She looked impressed with my artistic ability.

"Want one?" I asked.

She twirled her hair around her finger. "Not a pirate," she said. "I want a bumblebee."

"One itty-bitty bumblebee it is."

But it looked lonely, so I said, "How about I add some flowers?"

She nodded. So I grabbed all the markers and used a different one for each flower. By the time I finished, Miss Priss-A-Poo looked like a garden of daisies, delphiniums, and daffodils waiting to be picked.

Suddenly, Crockett pulled his sleeve over his tattoo and whispered, "Shiver me timbers."

I followed Crockett's gaze to . . . Mrs. Bingsley!

"Arrr . . ."

Was she trying to talk like a pirate?

"Wh . . . wh . . ."

"The 'arrr' was great, Mrs. Bingsley," I said politely. "But I don't think pirates say 'wh-wh.'"

That's when I noticed her grumpy, grumpy eyes and her red, red cheeks. She sure looked like she needed a happy face tattoo.

Mrs. Bingsley took a deep breath. "What are you doing with those *permanent* markers?"

Oops! I didn't realize I had been tattooing everyone with permanent markers. I tried to change the subject with a super-duper fun fact. "Mrs. Bingsley, did you know that there are 293 ways to make change for a dollar?"

Mrs. Bingsley pushed her sleeves up to her elbows and then folded her arms. She meant business.

My stomach felt fluttery. "Did you know that it's physically impossible to lick your elbow?"

Crockett wasn't the only one with a cool calendar. Mine was filled with 365 useless facts, which come in handy during times like this.

She took a deep breath then said, "Katharine, I asked you what you're doing with those *permanent* markers."

I eeked out, "Brainstorming?"

She snatched the marker out of my hand. "You mean fooling around?"

"I was practicing my tattoo drawing," I replied.

Mrs. Bingsley scrunched her face. "Use your common sense, Katharine. You can't draw on people." She put her hands on her hips. "What am I going to do with you?"

I thought of Dare to Be Different Day. "Um . . . maybe you should dare to be different and just . . . um . . . forget about it?"

I crossed my fingers. This is what I hoped would happen:

Mrs. Bingsley would say, "You're right, Katharine. Practicing your tattoo drawing is a great idea. Maybe you can tattoo an apple on my cheek?"

But this is what really happened:

She pointed toward the door.

Blimey! Forced to walk the plank . . . again!

## ❀ CHAPTER 2 ❀

### *Ammer the Hammer*

I went straight to the principal's office. Well, except for three drinks at the water fountain and a careful study of the utterly fab-u-lo-so front hall display.

The secretary, Mrs. Tracy, was on the phone, which was a-okay with me. Since I'm a frequent flier, I know the routine.

I ploppity plopped on the *green* chair by the window, not the *purple* chair by the phone. The first time I spied that purplicious chair, I ran over to it and bounced up and down until Mrs. Tracy got grumpy with me.

"That seat is off-limits," she said and pointed to the small table. "Teachers might need to sit *there* and use *that* phone."

But in all my visits here, I've never ever seen a teacher use the phone.

Visits. That's what I call my frequent-flier trips to see my principal, Mrs. Ammer. Kids call her *Ammer the Hammer* because she nails them for every little thing.

The first time I told my parents I visited her, my mom said, "A visit is when you go have milk and cookies with someone. Make no mistake about it, Katharine Marie Carmichael, you were *sent* to the principal's office."

If this were a movie, you'd see a flash of lightning and hear a boom of thunder when she said the word *sent*. Her thunder and lightning words make my stomach do a flip-flop belly drop.

Mom might feel better if she knew how totally educational my visits to Mrs. Ammer are. I have learned important school rules such as:

1. Do not use the principal's bathroom. If you do, *do not* use her expensive perfume as air freshener.

2. Do not call your grandmother to say, "hello."

3. When a button says, *In Case Of Fire, Press Here,* do not test it out to see if the fire department comes.

Mrs. Ammer finally buzzed Mrs. Tracy and told her to send me in. She was pouring herself a cup of coffee when I arrived. I looked to see if she had a plate of cookies anywhere. She didn't.

Mrs. Ammer stirred her coffee slowly with an orangey stick that was the same color as her hair.

"Ms. Carmichael, what a surprise." She pointed to the seat in front of her desk. "And to what do I owe this lovely visit?"

When she said the word *visit* I relaxed. She's not a scary principal to me. Still, I didn't want to talk about the tattoos.

"Did you know that only 4 percent of people in the world have naturally red hair?" I said.

"Interesting," she said as she fluffed her hair. "But getting back to my question . . . why are you here?"

"I'm trying to raise oodles and oodles of money. For charity."

"That seems honorable, Katharine. And what's the problem?" Mrs. Ammer said.

"There's no problem," I replied.

"And I suppose Mrs. Bingsley wasn't upset with you for doodling on your classmates?"

"Only three of them," I protested.

"And you felt the need to use your friends as an art canvas? I'm not surprised it upset my good friend, Mrs. Bingsley."

Now I was surprised. Mrs. Bingsley and Mrs. Ammer were good friends? Mrs. Bingsley freaked out when anyone started a sentence with the word *and*. Mrs. Ammer started most of her sentences that way!

"I just wanted to help the poor. Honest," I said.

Mrs. Ammer smiled. "You have a big heart, Katharine. You're a great kid."

"*Almost* great," I said. "My mom says I'm still a work-in-progress. I think I'll be great by the time I get to fourth grade."

"Maybe," she said. "Okay, Katharine the *Almost* Great, do you promise to use markers only on paper?"

I nodded.

"And I trust you'll apologize to all of your friends."

I thought of Miss Priss-A-Poo. She wasn't a friend. "Sure. To all of my friends."

Mrs. Ammer pursed her lips. "To anyone you drew on, Katharine. And that includes Vanessa."

There was the *and* again. Six times in two minutes. We'd be able to raise tons of money if we charged Mrs. Ammer one dollar for every sentence she started with the word *and*.

"And if you'd just use your common sense a little bit more," said Mrs. Ammer, "you might not get into so much trouble."

Seven times.

Silly Mrs. Ammer. Didn't she know I was using my common sense right now? I wasn't mentioning her use of the word *and*, was I?

Mrs. Ammer flashed another smile. This is what I thought would happen next:

Mrs. Ammer would say, "I'm going to have to call your parents again, Katharine. They're going to be very disappointed."

But this is what really happened:

Mrs. Ammer said, "There's no need to call your parents, Katharine. Your intentions were good. I think you learned a lesson."

Wow! I jumped up and hug-a-rooed Mrs. Ammer. I headed back to class promising never ever to draw on my classmates again. At least not in school.

## CHAPTER 3

### *Whipping Up an Idea*

"**A**mmer the Hammer's not calling your parents?" asked Crockett as we walked home from school. "You're luckier than a flea on a dog."

There are two things you should know about Crockett.

1. Crockett doesn't actually live with me. He lives below me. When his parents got divorced two years ago, he and Aunt Chrissy moved into our basement.

2. Crockett's real name is William. He says William is like vanilla ice cream: boring. So after he earned his Wilderness Survival Badge in Junior Rangers, he presto changed it to Crockett. As in Davy Crockett, King of the Wild Frontier.

According to him, this is what happened at camp:

1. He sucked venom out of his arm after a rattlesnake bit him.

2. He survived by eating nothing but tree bark and locusts for two days.

3. He walked four miles through a mosquito-infested swamp to find water to drink.

But Aunt Chrissy said that this is what really happened at camp:

1. He got stung by a bee and had to pull the stinger out.

2. He upchucked from eating too many s'mores.

3. He walked 50 feet to the snack bar to get bottled water.

Since Crockett was my cousin, my best friend, and a whole foot taller than me, I zipped my lips. Good-bye, William. Hello, Crockett.

As we reached our house, Crockett pointed to the gutter. "Look, Katharine. A penny."

His face lit up like he discovered a stack of hundred dollar bills. "I'm going to be rich one day."

"Pennies can't make you rich." Then I remembered the five pennies the lunch lady gave me for change. I reached into my pocket, pulled them out, and tossed them to him.

"Thanks!" He shoved them into his backpack. "You know what they say, *Save your pennies and your dollars will take care of themselves.* I bet I have at least $1,000 in my jars."

He scanned the gutter for more. Crockett exaggerates. A lot.

"You could see for yourself if you'd come downstairs."

I do not go into the basement. *Ever.* Not to see Crockett's pennies. Not to play his video games. Not to swing on the jungle boy rope he hung from his bedroom ceiling.

Crockett has all sorts of critters down there: snakes, a tarantula, lizards, and for all I know maybe even a T. rex. I think nature belongs *out*doors instead of *in* my basement.

I changed the subject. "Do you have any fund-raising ideas?"

"Nope, but Vanessa does. Her list is long."

I bet they all say car wash. Visions of her with a bucket and a sponge popped into my head. We'd have the car wash fund-raiser all over again if I didn't come up with an idea.

Crockett rubbed his stomach. "I'm starving." He licked his lips. "Does your mom have any cookies left?"

My mom's chocolate chip cookies were legendary. "Nope. Sorry."

Crockett looked bummed. "I'd give up all my pennies for one of those cookies right now."

That's when I got another idea. A much-better-than-tattoos idea. A better-than-any-Miss-Priss-A-Poo-idea idea.

"Crockett!" I shouted. "That's it! We can bake and sell cookies. We'll make millions."

Crockett nodded slowly. "You know what, Katharine? I think you're on to something here. I bet we could get a dollar a cookie."

Ten minutes later, we were in the kitchen whipping up our first batch with Aunt Chrissy.

Aunt Chrissy worked from home, so she babysat me whenever Mom had to run somewhere. Today, my baby brother, Jack, had a checkup.

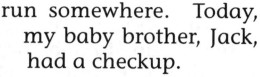

Crockett and I insisted we didn't need help. But Aunt Chrissy insisted that without her supervision, we could have major fire drama.

"I think this is a great idea," said Aunt Chrissy. "I'm glad to help out."

For the next hour, the three of us made four dozen chocolate chip cookies. Each time we made a new batch, we added extra chip-a-roos to the recipe.

"We make a good team," said Aunt Chrissy as she fished around for a spatula.

And we did. We arranged it like an assembly line in a factory. I poured the ingredients into the bowl and Crockett stirred the mixture. Then, Aunt Chrissy dropped the cookies onto the sheet and baked them.

After lots of dump, dump, STIR-STIR, dump, dump, dump, STIR-STIR, plop, plop, plop, they were finito!

Aunt Chrissy snatched the first cookie off the cooling rack.

"These are delicious," she said. She leaned in close. "Don't tell your mom, but these are even better than hers."

Just then, my mom walked in the door with Jack. "Well, well, what do we have here?"

Crockett told her all about our service project.

"I think it's the perfect fund-raiser," she said. "Just be sure to leave a few cookies here so I can put some in your father's lunch tomorrow."

Then, she looked around the room and sighed. Flour, cracked eggshells, measuring cups, and spoons were everywhere. A few chocolate chips had fallen on the floor. Vanilla had spilled on the counter. I knew what she was thinking: it looked as if a tornado had blown through a bakery.

I blurted out, "Did you know that cacao beans were used as money by Aztec and Mayan tribes?"

Mom opened her mouth. This is what I wanted her to say:

"You worked really hard on this fund-raiser, kids. Why don't you take some cookies and go watch TV before dinner. I'll clean up."

But this is what she really said:

"Katharine, you have fifteen minutes to clean up this mess before your father gets home. Crockett, you helped make this mess, so you can help clean it up, too. Aunt Chrissy is off duty."

She clapped her hands twice and thundered, "*Fifteen minutes!*"

After I cleaned the kitchen, Mom ordered me to clean my room. And Jack's room. And the dining room. And my bathroom.

Why? Because Miss Priss-A-Poo's mother called and told my mom all about my tattoo drawing.

*Ammer the Hammer* didn't nail me. Vanessa did.

And that was the end of my ick, make-me-feel-sick day.

## ❀ CHAPTER 4 ❀

### *That's the Way the Cookie Crumbles*

During snack time at school the next day, Crockett and I took our tin of cookies up to Mrs. Bingsley's desk.

"What do you have there, kids? I didn't miss one of your birthdays did I?" She glanced at the birthday train behind her desk.

"It's no one's birthday, Mrs. Bingsley," said Crockett. "But we do have a special treat for you and the class."

"Crockett and I worked hard baking these last night." I opened the lid, letting the chocolaty scent escape. "We were thinking we could sell these cookies for the fund-raiser. We wanted you to be the first to taste them. It's my mom's secret recipe."

Johnny's chocolate chip cookie radar revved up. He rushed up to Mrs. Bingsley's desk. "Oh, Katharine's mom makes the BEST cookies in the world!"

I beamed. "It's true."

Kids crowded around to get a better look. Mrs. Bingsley sniffed the air.

"They do smell wonderful," Mrs. Bingsley said. "My mouth's watering."

That's when we heard someone's stomach growl. Everyone laughed.

"Would you like one, Mrs. Bingsley?" I asked.

I was positive that once she ate one, her taste buds would explode-a-rama and do a happy dance. And then this is what would happen:

She'd rush to the intercom and call Mrs. Ammer and tell her to get down here this minute to taste the most fab-u-lo-so cookies in the world.

Then, Mrs. Ammer would run down and try one. And another and then another. She'd say, "These are divine" and ask if she could take some back to her office in case she had visitors.

Then, she'd call the newspaper. And, the newspaper would take a picture of Crockett and me baking the cookies.

But that's not what happened. This is what happened:

Mrs. Bingsley placed the cover over the tin and said, "As delicious as they look and smell, I'm afraid I can't have one. I'm lactose intolerant."

"Lact-what?" I asked.

"Lactose intolerant. It means I can't have milk or I'd get sick. Sorry, Katharine. Sorry, Crockett."

"I'm not lactose whatever," said Johnny. "Can I have one?"

Mrs. Bingsley shook her head. "Sorry, Johnny. I'm pretty sure I spied a few nuts in them."

Crockett and I looked at each other. How could we have forgotten Johnny's nut allergy?

"Sorry, Johnny," I said. "I promise I'll make some without nuts next time."

Tamara chimed in, "I can't have one either. I'm allergic to chocolate. I'd break out in a rash all over my body."

Then all the kids started talking.

Rebecca asked, "Do they have wheat? I can't have anything with wheat or I'll get a stomachache."

"What about eggs?" asked Matthew. "Did you use eggs? I blow up like a balloon if I even *look* at a chicken."

Mrs. Bingsley frowned.

"Guess what, Mrs. Bingsley," I said, trying to distract her from the kids. "The biggest chocolate chip cookie ever weighed 40,000 pounds and was over 102 feet wide."

But then Miss Priss-A-Poo just *had* to get in on the conversation. "Did any of your utensils come in contact with raw fish? I could die. D-I-E if anything touches raw fish."

I glared at Vanessa. Did she really think I made these cookies while my mom was preparing sushi?

Mrs. Bingsley tapped her desk. "Okay, everyone. Take two steps backward so no one gets squished." She took the tin of cookies from my hand.

"You both worked hard to make all of these, huh?"

We nodded.

"That was sweet of both of you. But with so many food allergies in here, I think it's best to avoid any food-related fund-raisers."

Poof. Just like that, my idea bit the dust. I marched over and sat on the purplicious beanbag chair to think.

A minute later, a tiny piece of folded paper sailed through the air and landed on my lap. I opened it up. It said:

That's the way the cookie crumbles.

–V.

I wanted to crumble Miss Priss-A-Poo.

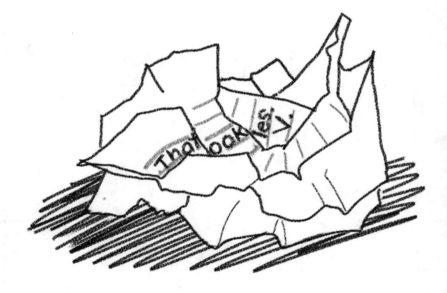

## ❀ CHAPTER 5 ❀

*Rent-a-Kid*

"I'm sorry your cookie idea didn't work out," said Dad. "I'm sure you'll think of another idea in no time."

I wasn't so sure. "It's already Friday night and I struck out with both ideas so far." I took a swig of milk. "I bet Miss Priss-A-Poo is going to have a zillion ideas on Monday morning."

Mom cleared her throat. I knew she was getting ready for a big speech.

"First of all, her name is Vanessa. Stop calling her Miss Priss-A-Poo. Second of all, it only takes one idea."

Jack was in his high chair drinking his bottle. I tickled his toes.

Dad wiped his mouth. "Don't lose sight of why you're having a fund-raiser, Katharine. It's to help people in need—*not* to duke it out with Vanessa to see who can top each other."

My throat felt all lumpy.

"Your father's right. It doesn't really matter who comes up with the best idea as long as the idea generates a lot of money," Mom added.

Of course I knew they were right. But I still wanted everyone to fuss over *my* idea. Last year, Vanessa and her family got *their* picture in the paper. *Her* name was announced over the intercom. *She* got a certificate with gold stars on it.

"Did you know that each person in the United States eats an average of 46 slices of pizza a year?" With that interesting fact, dinner was over.

After I cleared the table, I jumped up and down three times in front of the kitchen sink. That was my signal to Crockett that I was ready for movie night. Every Friday night I'd make the popcorn and he'd bring the movie.

A few minutes later, Aunt Chrissy yelled up the stairs, "Crockett has to bail on you, Katharine. He's not feeling well. I suspect he had more cookies than his stomach could handle."

The cookies were cursed!

Saturday started off just like any other Saturday. My parents dropped Crockett and me off at the YMCA for swimming lessons.

"You sure you want to be here?" I asked. "Do you still feel sick?"

Crockett burped. "I feel much better now. In fact, I could eat another cookie."

After our lesson ended, I went to the locker room to presto change out of my bathing suit. I felt a tap on my shoulder. I turned around to see my neighbor Melissa.

"How's Jack? I miss the little guy," she said. Melissa was Jack's babysitter whenever Aunt Chrissy couldn't watch him. She had been away for a month taking care of her sick father.

"He's still pretty much a little blob," I said. "He eats, poops, and sleeps. And then he does it all over again."

She patted her stomach. "Did your mom tell you that Mr. Jones and I are going to have our own baby in five months?"

I nodded. "Congratulations."

"I keep saying that I want a baby just as sweet as Jack. I wish your mom and dad would plan another date night so I could babysit him."

She put her hand on her hips. "You know, I'd pay them to let me babysit." She patted her belly again. "I could use the hands-on practice."

My wheels started turning.

"Melissa, would it be okay if I brought Jack by for a visit today? I think he'd love to see you, too. He's sitting up all by himself now."

"Oh, I'd love to see Jack. Why don't you come over around two o'clock? I'm going to recharge my camera batteries."

I, Katharine the *Almost* Great, got another idea. A better-than-drawing-tattoos idea. A better-than-baking-cookies idea. I couldn't wait to tell Crockett.

"I don't think it will work," said Crockett, shaking his head. "Your mom will never let you give Jack to Melissa."

"I'm not *giving* Jack to her. I'm *lending* him to her. That's all."

"She said she'd pay you? It doesn't make sense."

I explained how Melissa was having her own baby in five months and how she needed "hands-on" practice. And wouldn't Jack be the best practice she could get?

"If it works, maybe we could get everyone in our class to rent out their brothers and sisters to pregnant people."

I started thinking of all the kids in our class and counted all the siblings they had.

Crockett was thinking about it, too. "Johnny has three little brothers. He'd be able to make a lot of money off of them."

"Now you're thinking, Crockett. This will work."

At two o'clock sharp, I asked my mom if we could take Jack to visit Melissa. I promised to be home in one hour.

Mom said it was okay, so Crockett, Jack, and I left for Melissa's. It didn't take long to get there, since she only lives two houses away from us.

When we got there, Melissa scooped Jack up in her arms. "I've missed you, little guy." He cooed and kicked his feet.

Crockett said, "I think he missed you, too."

"Um, Melissa?  Do you think you could watch Jack for an hour?  Mom said it would be okay but . . ."

"But what?" she asked.

"Well, we want you to pay us since we're lending him to you so you can learn how to be a better parent," I said in a rush.

"You're charging me?  To watch Jack?" she said in amazement.

I looked at Crockett.  This wasn't going too well.  "You did say you'd pay big bucks to watch him since you missed him so much."

"True enough," said Melissa.  "How about ten dollars for the hour.  I'm sure Jack will teach me lots of stuff in sixty minutes."

Ten bucks!  This was easier than I thought!  Crockett gave me two thumbs-up.

I kissed Jack good-bye and high-fived Crockett when we got outside. "We did it! Rent-a-Kid is officially open for business."

Our super-duper celebration was short-lived. When we got back to Melissa's house an hour later, Mom was there waiting for us. I could tell she was going to be using *lots* of thunder and lightning words.

## ❀ CHAPTER 6 ❀

### *Common Cents!*

"Katharine, WHY DID YOU RENT JACK OUT TO MELISSA?" Ouch. Her thunder and lightning words were extra rumbly.

Melissa put her cup down. "Well, I did say I'd pay for baby practice." She mouthed *sorry* when my mom wasn't looking.

"Yep," I said. "Believe her. She did."

Jack was drooling, completely unaware that the big stink brewing wasn't his diaper.

Mom fumed. "That doesn't make it okay to RENT OUT YOUR BABY BROTHER!" She held out her hand. "Give me the money, Katharine."

Crockett reached into his pocket and took out a crumbly ten dollar bill.

I protested. "But, Mom . . . Melissa said she'd pay to learn from Jack. We had a deal. Fair and square. We think we'll make lots of money for the fund-raiser."

"The fund-raiser? I should have known. Do not bring Jack into any fund-raiser. You do *not* rent people. DVDs? Yes. Cars? Yes. Babies? *No!*"

She lifted Jack up and said, "Did you really think that moms and dads all over town would lend out their kids to complete strangers?"

Crockett whispered, "I knew it wasn't such a good idea."

"Katharine, you *must* use your common sense. There are a lot of crazy people in the world. You can't just go around giving away babies."

She looked at Melissa. "I'm just so glad that she picked you to hatch this silly plan with."

Mom pointed to the door. "Apologize to Melissa and both of you go straight home. You're both grounded."

I would have told her that she wasn't allowed to ground Crockett, but my common sense kicked in. That would have only gotten me into deeper trouble.

❀ ❀ ❀

The rest of the day was spent in my room. By myself. All alone. Mom knocked on the door at five thirty. This is what I wanted her to say:

"I'm sorry for overreacting, Katharine. After thinking about it, your father and I decided that I was wrong and you were right. To show you how truly sorry we are, we want to take you and Crockett out to dinner and a movie."

But this is what she really said:

"When you're done with your dinner, put the tray out in the hallway."

I've never, ever eaten dinner all by myself. Could this day get any worse? I didn't want to find out. I ate my dinner, brushed my teeth, and went to bed. At six thirty.

The next morning, Dad declared that my punishment was over. I waited until nine o'clock before jumping three times in front of the sink. A minute later, Aunt Chrissy came up.

"Crockett isn't allowed to come up and visit you today. I think we need to get through the rest of the weekend without the two of you cooking up any more fund-raising schemes."

She looked at my parents. "I really feel horrible about yesterday."

In case my parents decided I needed an extra day of punishment too, I changed the subject.

"Did you know that there are 2.7 billion packages of cereal sold every year? That's enough boxes to wrap around Earth 13 times." And then I skedaddled back up to my room.

School was tomorrow and I had zilch. Nada. No ideas to share. And to make it an extra stink-o-rama day, I couldn't see Crockett.

I turned on my computer and saw I had a new e-mail. I knew it was from Crockett because he's the only one I've given my e-mail address. I quicky quick opened it up.

*Katharine,*

*I'm sorry we both got in trouble. Are you punished for two days? We still have today to think up a cool fund-raiser. If I think of one, I'll let you know. I took some pictures of my animals and my room since you're too chicken to come down here.*

*Crockett*

Was he kidding? I was out of ideas. I figured Miss Priss-A-Poo had it wrapped up again. I clicked on the pictures.

The first picture was of the tarantula crawling on Crockett's arm. A chill went up my spine. I sure hoped it was back in its cage. I pressed delete.

The second picture was of Aunt Chrissy making cookies. Ugh!

The third picture was of Crockett folding laundry. Under it, he wrote: Crockett's Punishment.

The fourth picture was of a bunch of five gallon water jugs. It said, "Since you won't come look at all my pennies, I sent you this picture."

I leaned closer to the screen. Were all those coppery dots really pennies? He must have millions of them!

I looked around my room. A few dozen pennies were in my Mets cup and a few hundred were in my piggy bank.

My mind raced. Dad had a milk jug full of pennies in his closet. Mom had a few baby jars full in the kitchen. I had a lightbulb moment and danced around my room.

I had figured out the perfect fund-raiser! Mom, Mrs. Ammer, and Mrs. Bingsley sure would be proud of me. I, Katharine the *Almost* Great, was finally using my common *cents*!

## ❀ CHAPTER 7 ❀

### *Mucho Mega Moola*

I dashed down the steps into the kitchen. Aunt Chrissy was having toast and coffee with my parents.

"Slow down," said Dad. "What's the rush?"

I spoke super-duper fast. "Aunt Chrissy, I know Crockett isn't supposed to come up here today, but can I go downstairs for a quicky quick minute?"

She frowned. "I don't know."

"Please? It's a matter of life and death."

Aunt Chrissy buttered another piece of toast. "Life or death? It must be if you're willing to brave those creepy critters in the basement." Then she looked up sharply.

"What?" I asked in my very most innocent voice.

Aunt Chrissy pointed her buttered toast at me. "No cooking up wild schemes. No baby rentals. No turning our street into a toll road. No charging people not to have Crockett's tarantula dropped down their shirts. Got it?"

I was amazed. We should have had Aunt Chrissy come up with ideas before. Those were great! I bet Miss Priss-A-Poo would pay big bucks to keep a tarantula out of her clothes. But then I'd have to get awfully close to the tarantula.

"Katharine . . .," Mom said in her I'm-warning-you voice.

"Got it!" I said. My idea was better anyway. "Is that a yes?"

Mom glanced at Aunt Chrissy. "It's fine with me if it's okay with you."

"I should warn you," said Aunt Chrissy. "Crockett's feeding crickets to the lizards."

I swallowed hard and told myself to be brave. This would be worth it. I just knew it.

"Crockett!" I yelled as I zip-a-zoomed down the stairs. "CROCKETT!"

He poked his head out from the kitchen. "Katharine! This is a first. What are you doing down here?"

The baggie in his hand was moving. "Wh . . . What's in there?"

He shoved his hand behind his back. "Trust me, you don't want to know. I'll be right back."

I walked into their living room and saw two tanks on the table. I was pretty sure the tarantula and snakes lived in them. I wasn't about to find out.

I hurried into the dining room. One glance around the room told me all I needed to know: lizards ruled the dining room.

"Crockett," I whined. "Is there any room that's critter-free? I can't stay

down here and see all of these . . . things."

"The bathroom is an animal-free zone. So is my mom's room. Let's go in there."

I sure was glad that Crockett wasn't the type of kid who would try to freak you out with his animals and bugs when he knew you were scared. I could trust him.

I sat on Aunt Chrissy's bed scanning the floor for any possible creepy crawlers. Once he promised the coast was clear, I took a deep breath.

"Okay. Where are they?" I demanded.

"The animals? They're all . . ."

"No, Crockett. The pennies! *Your* pennies. I can't believe you have so many. I bet you have zillions of dollars in those jug-a-roos."

"I knew you didn't believe me. I have three full jugs in my room and my mom has one almost full in here."

He slid the closet door open to reveal a dozen pairs of shoes neatly lined up on the floor.

"Oops. Wrong side." He slid the door in the opposite direction. I jumped off the bed.

"Crockett, you were right. You said if you save your pennies then your dollars will take care of themselves."

He nodded. Then I told him all about my plan.

"Do you think it will work?" asked Crockett. "Will the class go for it?"

"Of course they will. It's the most per-fect-o idea in the whole wide world."

I grabbed a piece of paper off of my aunt's nightstand. "Let's make a list of all the things we need to do to get ready for our presentation tomorrow and then get to work."

"What's all the buzz about?" asked Aunt Chrissy. She was standing in the doorway with my parents.

We told them all about our plan. They listened quietly as we explained how this would be the best fund-raiser of all.

Aunt Chrissy gave us a round of applause. Dad said he was just thrilled it didn't involve renting Jack out to strangers. Mom didn't say anything.

"What do you think, Mom?" My stomach got that shaky feeling. "Did you know that 30 million pennies are made each day?"

She peered into the jug and then kneeled in front of it.

This is what I thought she'd say:

"Katharine, you are too preoccupied with this fund-raiser. I'm still in shock about yesterday. I've been thinking it over. One day of punishment was not enough. You're going to have to stay in your room until you're 18."

But this is what she really said:

"I think that Mrs. Bingsley is lucky to have two thoughtful, caring, and hardworking kids in her class. I'm proud of both of you." She glanced at Aunt Chrissy and Dad. "We're all proud of you."

The five of us spent the next few hours emptying and counting all the pennies from Aunt Chrissy's five gallon jug.

The grand total: $498.32.

"Wow!" I yelled. "That's a lot of moola."

"If we multiply that by four—one for each jug—we have even more money," said Crockett as he punched numbers into a calculator. "That's $1,993.28!"

I screamed. "That's mucho mega more moola!"

We had the plan. We were ready for our presentation. Nothing could stop us now.

Except Miss Priss-A-Poo.

# ❀ CHAPTER 8 ❀

## *Drumroll, Please*

"We've had five wonderful ideas so far," Mrs. Bingsley said the next day. "Does anyone else have a suggestion?"

Crockett and I raised our hands. So did Miss Priss-A-Poo.

"Vanessa," said Mrs. Bingsley, "please share your idea first."

Vanessa walked to the front of the room. I crossed my fingers, arms, and legs. I even crossed the two pencils in my desk. I figured we needed all the luck we could get.

"I decided that we should *not* try to raise money for the poor next month."

The class got all buzzy and squirmy. Mrs. Bingsley took her glasses off and bit her lower lip. Miss Priss-A-Poo smiled. She couldn't fool me. I knew she was up to something.

"I was going to say we should do the car wash again because we *did* raise the most money EV-er last year."

She picked up a piece of chalk and walked to the board. She wrote FOOD BANK in large letters. "But then I visited the Food Bank with my Girl Scout troop on Saturday. They're running out of food and need more."

Mrs. Bingsley smiled and nodded.

"So, instead of raising money I thought we could bring in food and donate it to the Food Bank." She bowed. Everyone clapped.

"Another good idea and a different approach," said Mrs. Bingsley. "I like that."

My stomach did another flip-flop belly drop. We were doomed! I pressed too hard on one of my pencils, and it snapped in half.

"Crockett and Katharine, you're up," said Mrs. Bingsley.

I took a deep breath and brought our posters to the front of the room. Crockett went to the coatroom and got the empty five gallon jug he brought from home.

"How many of you have pennies collecting dust at your house?" asked Crockett.

Hands shot up into the air. Johnny called out, "I have about 20 right now."

"Twenty isn't much, is it?" I asked. "But if your friend has some . . ."

I turned to Crockett. "Do you have any?" I asked, pretending I didn't know about the stash in his pocket.

Crockett pulled 25 out and gave them to Johnny. "Now you have almost 50¢ and could buy a pack of gum," said Crockett. "Mrs. Bingsley, I notice that you have a jar of pennies on your desk. How many are in there?"

As she began counting the pennies, kids started searching through their pencil cases and backpacks. I passed around a cup to collect them. After adding up everyone's pennies, we had $3.34.

"Do you see how quickly pennies add up? One or two by themselves isn't much."

"But put them together . . .," added Crocket, then he unrolled his poster and held it up.

Everyone read the poster out loud,

"Save your pennies and your dollars will take care of themselves."

We lifted the five gallon jug onto Mrs. Bingsley's desk.

"I've been collecting pennies for a long time," said Crockett. "Yesterday, this jug was full of pennies. We counted them. Guess how much money was inside?"

Kids started guessing all sorts of amounts. Finally, Mrs. Bingsley held up her hand. That was her signal to settle down.

"Drumroll, Crockett." Crockett beat his hands against the empty jug.

"Crockett had $498.32 inside."

The class couldn't believe it.

"That's so cool!" said Johnny.

Vanessa looked unimpressed. "Katharine isn't very good at math. I bet she added it up wrong."

I gave Miss Priss-A-Poo the evil eye. "Crockett and I added them up . . . twice."

I waved toward the door. Everyone turned to see who I was waving to. The door opened and Aunt Chrissy and Mom walked in pulling a wagon full of pennies.

I announced all dramatic-like, "This is what $498.32 looks like."

Everyone rushed to get a closer look. We told them all about the four water jugs and how we could put empty jugs in each classroom and around town in popular places like the Pizza Palace and the movie theater.

"I have one more thing to say," said Crockett. I looked at him. We didn't practice a one-more-thing-to-say part.

"If we decide to have this penny fund-raiser, my mom and I want to donate all $498.32 of these pennies."

The class applauded.

Mrs. Bingsley gushed, "That's so generous of your family."

This is what I wanted her to say next:

"There's no need to vote. Crockett and Katharine's idea is the best idea I've ever heard in my whole entire life. They should win a major award."

But this is what she really said:

"We'll vote after lunch."

And that's what we did. By super-duper secret ballot. Mrs. Bingsley called us over to the carpet to announce the results.

"Class, there were so many wonderful ideas presented today. Please remember that our goal is to show how caring the students at Liberty Corner School are. We want to help contribute to society and make the world a better place."

Whoa! I didn't know we were doing all that! I felt extra important and sat up extra tall.

"We have a tie," said Mrs. Bingsley. "It looks like we'll be collecting pennies and collecting food for the Food Bank."

Crockett and I jumped up and down. Miss Priss-A-Poo jumped up and down. Then, she jumped over Johnny and jumped up and down with us.

"You should put a jar at the library," said Miss Priss-A-Poo. "Lots of people go there. And lots of people eat at Wing Li's Chinese Restaurant. Put one there, too."

She was going to help us? "Thanks, Miss Pr . . . Vanessa. Maybe the Pizza Palace and Wing Li's can donate food to the Food Bank. We should ask them."

A minute later, Mrs. Bingsley pointed to the door. "Go tell Mrs. Ammer what our class fund-raisers are."

Vanessa bit her lip and clutched my arm. "She's sending us to *Ammer the Hammer*?"

"Don't worry," I said. "We're just visiting."

# *Raise Funds* and *Have Fun*

Fund-raisers can earn mucho mega moola for your school or community and show that you care!  Follow these steps to plan your fund-raiser:

(1) Decide what you want to raise money for. Do you want to build a new playground for your school, help people in your community, or raise money for someone in need?

(2) Decide what you want do to raise money.  You could have a walk-a-thon, sell food, or ask for donations.  Be creative, and think FUN!

(3) Figure out who can get involved. Can you ask school workers, parents, and local businesses to help?

(4) Gather the supplies you'll need and start raising money!  Helping a good cause will make you feel great and show you care.